THE PUD

CW00506725

Brilliant, another day walking home in the rain, at least its only spitting, it was a good job the rain stopped just as I finished work, so I must be thankful for that.

Not a bad day, can't complain, made a load of money for the company and its looking good for my bonus at the end of the month, it's on days like this I think of what a good company I work for, staff are ok, although the boss, David, can be a pain in the neck sometimes, I even managed to get away half an hour early.

Suddenly a car rushes by me at speed and breaks my thought, then a screech of brakes as the car slides across the rain soaked tarmac, it hits the wall along the side of the old school, I run towards it ,but it bursts into flames, the driver screams, a long blood curdling scream ,I can feel the heat ,I throw my briefcase down and cover my head with my wet jacket, I still can't get near it, the flames are too fierce, I step back a few paces in case the fuel tank explodes, the tyres pop, one by one.

From where I'm standing ,I can hear the roar of the flames and the drivers screams and a strange noise, like squeaky voices, like the Cadbury's smash Martian's television advertisment from the 1970's, but where was it coming from, it was everywhere. Just squeaky voices then laughing, weird, squeaky almost frightening laughter, filled the air ,then nothing,! perhaps it's the wind I thought, but then silence, just the sound of my own heavy breathing, I look around and was thinking aloud," what the hell happened there".? my mind was racing ,I get my mobile out to phone the emergency services ,damn, no service, the puddles were not that deep, so it wouldn't cause the car to aquaplane and it couldn't be ice in august, It's just as though someone or something just lifted the car out of the puddle and pushed it away.

I shook myself, bloody hell that's weird, I try again to get service and make the call, but I can already hear the sounds of the sirens, fire brigade and ambulance then the police arrived, but they can do nothing for the man inside the car.
The fire brigade quickly put out the flames, the ambulance crew just wait, they too,can do nothing, one of the police, a tall Sergeant walks over to me,"

excuse me sir my name is Sergeant Ford, did you see what happened ", there's concern in his voice.

I hesitated, then said " well yes, umm, well not really ", which is it sir, did you witness the accident or not, I don't think he was impressed with my answer.

I shouted at the sergeant, " Shhh listen", we were both quiet," I'm listening for" the sergeant asked, I answered," there's no wind"," no there isn't" said the sergeant, now agitated by the whole situation, he takes a step closer as I watch the fire service put out the last of the flames.

Did you, or did you not witness the accident, " well yes ", I answered in a rather timid voice," only you don't seem to sure he added ".

" That's because I'm not" , the sergeant raises an eyebrow.

Feeling pressured to say something , I tell the truth, " all I know was the Citroen coming down the road, past me and as soon as his wheels touched the puddle the car sort of jumped across the road and burst into flames when it hit the wall",," sort of jumped " the sergeant said, writing ' excess speed/ aquaplaned, into his notepad.

After giving my name and address details I was ok to go, with the sergeant giving me a card with his name on it, I turned, took two steps and the strange voices started again, but just laughing this time, I spun round to ask the sergeant if he could hear them but he was already in his car and showing no real concern for the situation, after all, it was just an accident wasn't it.?

I went home, still pondering the voices.
I told Michelle (my wife) about the accident as soon as I got in, but didn't mention the voices for fear of getting laughed at ,but as I tried to put the day's events to the back of my mind, I had this thing bugging me, what made the car jump so violently.? and the voices, was I just hearing things.?

I played monopoly with the children,(Toni and Tom), before they went to bed, I lost the game, my mind still thinking about the accident ,I then done the day's paperwork and headed up the stairs to bed.

The next morning was bright, with beautiful sunlight shining through the windows early, I'll have a better day today, I thought, I'm sure of it.

I had breakfast, kissed the kids and Michelle goodbye and headed off to work.

With the events of the previous day still playing heavy on my mind, I was glad to see that most of the ground had dried up and very few puddles remained.

Everyone in the office greeted me with the normal smile except the boss (David), " god, you look rough, bad night was it." he said, " cheers then " I said sarcastically and walked into my own office.

I finished work as normal and was looking forward to my fish and chips, after all, it was a Friday and that was the norm, as I walked home I pondered on the day's events, another good day, made the firm a load of money, everything felt good, it didn't last long though, as it started to rain it made me think of the previous day, hell, this is driving me mad I thought and as I got nearer home it started to rain harder, I heard the voices again, the same as the previous day, only no laughter, the squeaky voices were saying something but it was too difficult to make out what they were saying. " got it ", I said out loud as I pushed open the front gate, they were saying "another one today ".

" Got what " Michelle said as I walked through the front door, " oh, nothing " I said, but I don't think she believed me, after 25 years of marriage I think she could tell when I was lying, " suit yourself " she said.

The rain began to get harder, beating noisily on the conservatory roof, but above the noise I could hear the siren of one of the emergency services, although I didn't know which one, as they all sound the same to me.

My mind drifted back to the day before, it couldn't happen again, could it.?
My question was quickly answered, the house at number 22 had a kitchen fire, so it was the fire brigade, the rain eased, just as the fire tender pulled up and, with the normal professionalism disaster was averted.

The puddles were deep outside number sixteen, with a mix of water from the fire truck and rain water, with one puddle stretching right across the road, the children from across the street were happily trying to jump the width of the puddle until one, the youngest, about seven years of age, seem to trip and fall head long into the deepest part, I ran over and scooped him up , it was Brian, from across the road, he was soaked from to head to toe and had blood running down his face from a nasty cut above his left eye.

I was stood in the puddle while frantically trying to get my mobile out of my back pocket, at the same time still holding the child, I tapped out 999 and went through the procedure of telling the lady on the other end I needed an ambulance then gave her my address and details she needed.

I said " hurry it looks really bad "I was not trained in first aid but had watched enough TV to know what I had to do.

As I carried him back to my house his mother who we knew as Dawn came running out of her house screaming to her child " Brian, Brian" she shouted several times, " the ambulance is on its way "I said trying to settle her," Brian, Brian", she was calling to her child as his eyes started to roll, we heard the siren of the ambulance service just as Brian started to go limp in my arms," no, no", I shouted, Dawn was now screaming hysterically.

I started CPR as soon as I led Brian down on our lawn and continued until the ambulance crew took over, it seemed like a life time but we got Brian breathing again.

Within a minute, Brian was in the ambulance along with Dawn and on their way to hospital, after another minute, I got over the shock of what happened and walked over to the puddle, there was no reason why Brian should have tripped, but hey, he is a child, they do that don't they.?

I walked back home feeling saddened, thinking I could have done more, but then, possibly, I did save his life, just like yesterday my life is being turned upside down by anything connected with water.

For god's sake, what am I thinking, I'm getting paranoid, over two things that are not even related, just coincidences .

The day ended with a feeling of happiness, as the phone rang about 10pm, I recognised the number," hi Dawn", I said, trying to stay cheerful" you ok".? I was fearing the worst," we're just on our way to bed, how's Brian".?

"Brian's ok, thank you for saving his life", Dawn said," I'm sure you would have done the same" I replied.," anyway, just thought you would like to know thanks again , goodnight" and then Dawn hung up.

Michelle said a few words about how it seemed an eventful day as we got into bed, we then cuddled up close and went to sleep.

Dawn woke me with a shout," quick, there's been an accident", I looked out the bedroom window, there was a car in the middle of the road on its roof.

As I hastily put my clothes on and headed for the door I caught sight of the alarm clock, it was about twenty minutes to midnight, something was bugging me about the time but I couldn't remember what it was.

I remembered as I got outside and saw the car, 'another one today', the voices said earlier ,no, please no, I thought don't let it be. a lifeless body half under the car, it looked like he had the window open and was driving without a seatbelt, I felt sick, as I noticed a large pool of blood had formed and was starting to trickle down the camber of the road to meet the puddle.

In the distance I could hear the engine of the ambulance, then I saw the blue lights, but it was too late, the youngster was already dead, you could just feel it.

Another life lost and he too, just drove through a puddle, the ' hands ' of the puddle must have just pushed the car away just as it did the day before and also perhaps Brian too.

More laughter from the mysterious voices but they stopped as the ambulance crew arrived. The younger of the crew, a young girl that seemed barely twenty years old, looked, then looked away, she too, looked like she was going to be sick.

The police arrived and along with them the recovery crew, while the police cordoned off the area, the recovery team went about attaching harness to the car and began lifting the car away from the lad that lay beneath the wreckage.

The police finished and began walking over, my first thoughts were, " here we go again " and strangely enough it was the same sergeant as yesterday.

That's a coincidence he said, two accidents and you're at both of them,
"I was in bed", I quickly said, again, I gave him the details of what I saw but then I said. " there's a lot of water about again, " that there is, he said, that there is."

That was it, after a quick look at the car, which by then was being hoisted onto the recovery truck the sergeant went on, I looked across to the ambulance to see the crew lift the stretcher into the back with a sheet over the dead lads upper body.

I sat down on the wet pavement alone in the dark and put my head in my hands, well no weird voices or laughter this time, perhaps the reason why I couldn't hear any was because I was not alone," are you ready for bed " Michelle asked quietly, " uh, oh yes", I replied and got up, I took one last look at the puddle before I went through our front door and I could have sworn the puddle was moving.

I woke to the alarm the next morning, but feeling I could have done with another hour, but got up anyway, showered and went down for breakfast.

Michelle was silent, she had not told the kids the troubles of the night before, I too said nothing, it was an eerie silence, I kissed Michelle and the kids goodbye after breakfast and went out the door, I immediately I looked across to where the puddle lay, it was almost gone, I thought nothing more about it.

Into the office I strolled trying to feel awake and totally with it, only to be greeted today with no smiles, just strange looks, I looked at David," wow", he said, must have been some party. I went straight into the washroom, I can't look that bad, can I? I did, I aged overnight and what was that, a grey hair.?

The day went well as did the next day and a good feeling came over me, while thinking about the weekend.

In the evenings we sat and watched TV.
I woke about eight the next morning, Michelle had left a note saying she was walking the dog, I looked in on the kids, Tom was playing his laptop and Toni was still asleep.
Michelle came in just as reached the kitchen," tea dear", I asked, "yes please" she said," it's getting cold and it looks like it's going to rain", she continued, I dropped the kettle which was full, the handle broke and spewed water everywhere, " the cloth is in the cupboard " Michelle said as she bent down to pick up the pieces, " well we know what we're doing this morning, looking for a new kettle ", she said out loud.
" Shall we take the car" ?, Michelle said, after breakfast," no " I said aloud," lets walk today, it will do us good." Michelle was amazed as I only walk to work, with a struggle.

"I am so unfit "I said, as we got nearer the town centre shops, "well it will do us good", Michelle said sarcastically, we went in three shops and I'm sure we came away with the most expensive kettle, that'll teach me to be so jumpy when I hear the word rain. We got half way home and the heavens opened, heavy rain almost straight away and a black ford galaxy with blacked out windows didn't help by driving through a puddle and getting me soaked, I felt Michelle was watching me as I walked round every puddle, "you ok" she asked," yes, I just don't want to get my feet wet", I replied," bit late for that she said".

We stayed in for the rest of the day, doing nothing in particular, I looked out the windows to the puddles in the street, " the puddles seem to be moving " I said," but there's no wind ".

"have you ever noticed the puddles move when it rains" I asked, "yes of course they do , the rain causes ripples and the puddles get bigger", she replied, "yes of course," I said.

"Dad, dad, quick" said Tom. and we all rushed outside to see Dawn trying to sweep the puddles away, it was still just about raining and as dawn swept so the water would rush back to the same place, just like sweeping leaves in the wind.

Dawn was using foul language as she swept and it was difficult to understand her.

"steady", Michelle said, " there's no need for that with kids around".

" You don't know" she shouted," you just don't know," " can't you hear them", then came another line of expletives , we told the kids to go home while we tried to reason with Dawn.

Dawn threw the brush down on the floor and sunk slowly down to her knees in the middle of the puddle, she was incoherent , blubbering something about the people from the puddles.

It dawned on me that the strange squeaky type voices can be heard by other people too, but I said nothing in front of Michelle, both myself and Michelle helped Dawn walk back the few paces to her house, by now we were all soaked, but I must say, there was something sexy about Dawn being soaked with just jeans and t-shirt on.

We left Dawn at her front door and as Michelle turned and walked down Dawns path, I held Dawns hands, looked her in the eyes and whispered, " I know, I hear the voices and laughter too", I then turned and followed Michelle home.

We never heard from Dawn for the rest of the day, but in the morning, we had a party invite put through our letterbox for the same day and on the top of the invite the words, thank you.

We were the only ones invited to the impromptu party, with Brian still in hospital and his father Barry, (Dawns husband) away in Afghanistan.

" Do you think she's, well you know", said Michelle, as we were about to leave home," I don't think she's going mad if that's what you mean ",I replied sympathetically .
Dawn greeted us with a smile, she looked fantastic and younger than her 40 years, it is surprising what a bit of make-up and a smile can do.

Eventually as the evening went on and the wine started to take its toll, Dawn started to tell her stories of the voices she keeps hearing, "you need a holiday Dawn", Michelle said," I don't need a bloody holiday" came the reply ,there was silence for what seemed like an eternity, but in reality it was probably no more than a minute.

" It's getting late " Michelle eventually said," yes , it's been a long day," I said reluctantly , Michelle got up first, gave Dawn a hug and mentioned we are across the road if needed.

" I'll just finish this glass, I'll be there in a sec", I said as Michelle left and as soon as the door closed I held Dawns hands and looked her in the eyes, " I have heard the voices and laughter but I've not told Michelle yet, we've got to try to understand why this is happening," I was proud that I was so rational, it was so unlike me.

"We must try and put a stop to what is happening," but these", I paused, choosing my phrase carefully, "puddle people are causing mayhem, I will see you tomorrow, take care and stay safe", with a kiss on her soft cheek I went home.

Michelle was already in bed when I got home," you were quick" I said, there was no response, it had been a long day and a glass or two of wine always made Michelle sleepy.

The next morning was a bank holiday, we both had a lie in till about half eight, "where shall we go today "I said at breakfast, both Tom and Toni (brother and sister) both said " lets hit the beach " ," again," I said despairingly, " we always go to the beach", Michelle agreed with the kids,,, damn, I was outnumbered, I felt myself fearing for our lives due to the obvious large expanse of water, then I thought to myself ,I must get a grip.

" Ok, as soon as your ready then" I said reluctantly and within ten minutes we were on our way.

Can we go on a jet-ski" Tom asked," sounds good to me , maybe one each", I was trying to reassure myself all would be ok, after all, it's not a puddle is it and you don't hear ships just jumping out of the water.

After a full day building sandcastles, jet skiing and over indulging on seafood it was time to go, feeling happy with myself we had a good family day out on a day off.

We got home late and as the kids went straight to bed, Michelle packed away the beach things and I began to draw the curtains, as I did I caught sight of Dawns lounge light on, I wanted to go over and see if everything was ok, but it was obvious that it was not the right thing to do.

There was a gentle tap on the door, Michelle opened it to find Dawn asking for me," of course", Michelle said," come in " Dawn came straight into the lounge and immediately asked if I could help her after work

tomorrow level her drive, I looked at Michelle then said " yes "," it's just patching up" she said, it shouldn't take too long", " no worries" I said.
I walked into the office the next day and felt like a new man, no strange looks and no stupid comments from the boss.

After a full day, I looked forward to getting home and helping Dawn, to get stuck in to some real physical work .

As Dawn was working I questioned her why the need to fill in all the holes and cracks, the answer should have been clear to me, " I don't want to be anywhere where the puddle people can get us " she said.

Dawn was scared and it did make me worry for her safety.
How long before Barry is home from Afghanistan" I asked," about another six weeks" she said, " and I'm telling him that this is the last time, I need a man, I can't go on any longer without a man in my life," Dawn was looking straight at me.

Was she making a pass at me.? it felt good, but I said," you're just going through a bad patch, I'll help you till Barry gets home," I reassured her, " great, as long as Michelle doesn't mind." "she'll be fine, by the way, how's Brian", I said," their keeping him in for a couple more days" Dawn said, then we both stood back to admire our handiwork, we looked up at the dark clouds and wondered if there would still be puddles.!

"We can't fill every crack and hole in the village" I said, "well it's a start" replied Dawn, "anyway it's time for me to go and have a shower" I said , I'll come and scrub your back if you like" Dawn said," yes I would like that", I said, trying to play her at her own game, I then I picked up the tools and walked across the road to my own house, packed the tools in the shed and went in the back door.

Just as I got in Michelle was waiting for me, "Toni and Tom have gone down the village hall, they will be back at ten and I'm off to slimming club"," ok, I'm going to take a shower then sit down with a beer, the Italian job is on and I'm quite partial to a bit of Charlize Theron", Michelle laughed before saying " in your dreams", while giving me a kiss and heading out the door.

It was about half seven and my thoughts were shower, beer then film.

I started to undo my shirt and had only taken two steps up the stairs and Michelle had been gone less than five minutes when there was a gentle tap on the door, " sod it, now what " I said aloud.

I opened the door to Dawn, she looked stunning in a little black number, her long blonde hair still wet where she had already taken a shower and you could easily tell she was bra less.

"Hello" I said," what can I do for you", "well there's an offer" she said, looking at my unbuttoned shirt, "I've come to scrub your back she said," umm, yes", I said, I didn't mean to lead her on but I was testing her to see how far she would really go. Dawn followed me upstairs, "this isn't right", I said as I walked into the bedroom, " relax nobody's home" Dawn replied.

We went into the bedroom and as I turned round towards her she looks so good I just lost control, not sure whether I was just teasing her or loving the attention, I held her and we kissed, a full on passionate kiss, she rubbed against me and felt the bulge of my response, I felt the top of her dress and found the zip, then pulled it slowly to the bottom of her spine, I slipped her dress off her shoulders and saw her pert breasts and held one in each hand, warm and firm with nipples erect, we carried on kissing and her hands found my belt buckle, she started to undo it.

My mind was racing, I should stop this but it felt so good,. then suddenly... Dawn shouted, " what's that , rain, rain on the windows, no , no" Dawn said and started to cry, I tried to reassure it would be ok, but it was no good, in one quick movement she picked her dress up off the floor and was putting it on as she left the comfort of the bedroom, I called to her to wait, but it was in vain.

Not knowing what to do next, I got undressed and had my shower, I was still in my bath robe when Michelle came home, watching the last few minutes of the film I said " she is one sexy lady ", referring to Charlize Theron , " well, I'm getting there" Michelle said," I lost another three pounds this week", "that's great", I said and gave her a hug, it felt good, but I felt guilty at the same time, "I've missed you" I whispered, "I've missed you too", she said .
"Is it still raining " I asked," not really, just a bit of drizzle", came the reply.

Toni and Tom came home shortly after ten with tales of an accident on the other side of the village," it was a nice car dad" Tom said," looked like a BMW x5" , "what happened", I asked, fearing the answer," it looks like she was going to fast" Tom continued, "go on", I said, Toni jumped in with her opinion," she wasn't going to fast, don't be so sexist just because it was a woman driver, the lady was driving through a puddle when the car aquaplaned that's all."
I would say that's a bit unlikely as an BMW x5 weighs about two tonnes," I said.
" Its school tomorrow and you know what that means", Michelle said, " yes, time for bed " we all said together.

The alarm went off as normal at seven," I could have done with another hour" I said, " I could have done with another five or six", Michelle replied.
"You were so restless last night, have you anything on your mind", she asked.?
"nope, don't think so" 'I answered.

Of course I did, Dawn and the night before, the new car accident and David will probably tell me to go home because I look so rough," why don't you take the day off ",Michelle said," you do look tired"," cheers then" I said," but I could take a day as holiday" I continued.

I picked up the phone and dialled the works number, it rang once and I slammed the phone down, " shit" I said aloud David drives an x5, but it couldn't be, could it.?

I didn't have to wait long for the answer, the phone rang almost immediately , I answered it cautiously.

"Good morning, could I speak to tony please" the man sounded serious, " yes, speaking", I replied,, this is Sergeant Ford at the police station", he said," yes, how can I help", I said, it seemed the obvious response.

"Would you come down to the station this morning to help us with some of our enquiries", he asked, "yes, of course, what is it in connection with and any particular time ?, I said in a nervous tone ,"no just when you free" he said, I agreed and he hung up.

I was always a law abiding person so I had nothing to feel guilty about, but Michelle became suspicious asking several questions followed by" you must have done something wrong".

I rang the office reception and left a message for David, the secretary had just got in and knew nothing of the events of the night before, or perhaps it was a coincidence the car was the same.

I arrived at the police station around twenty past eleven and was taken to an interview room where the officer gave his name ,his number, the date, time and my name , then in one go pressed the two buttons on the recorder.

The officer starting asking questions about my whereabouts last night, asking if anyone could substantiate where I had been, I had to say no, to protect Dawn and my marriage ,
I was questioned on why I was in the vicinity of so many alleged accidents, I said I didn't know, it seemed strange to me too, then he started asking questions about my relationship with David Hurst," he's my boss "I said aloud, I was beginning to get annoyed with the questioning and how long they wanted me for, "settle down" the officer said.
The police officer finally told me that it was David that was involved in the accident and he was in intensive care, it was lucky he was in such a heavy car or he would have been killed, he said," what happened" I asked, as if I didn't already have a good idea.

" Well, his wife was driving as they had been to the new Indian restaurant in the centre of the village and Mr Hurst had been drinking and according to witness reports , as the car turned the corner of the high street into south street Mrs Hurst lost control when the car aquaplaned and hit the bus stop resulting in the top of the bus stop going through the windscreen and consequently putting Mr Hurst in intensive care and killing his lovely wife.

"She's dead, oh my god, they were the perfect couple, I need to phone work, for Christ's sake , how could they do this to such nice people"." do you know something we don't sir, who are they", " sorry" I said," I was thinking aloud, I meant the powers that be, you know, the gods or whatever".

The sergeant looked at me as though I had something to hide.

It was about half two when I finally left the police station and was about to go to work when I changed my mind and decided to go straight round to Dawns Instead, I knocked on the door and went in," sorry about last night" Dawn said from the top of the stairs," the rain really freaks me out now, I keep thinking who the hell next" "well I can answer that one I said, as I started to walk up the stairs.

I carried on talking as I reached Dawn," it was my boss, an accident at south street" ,"and" Dawn asked fearing the answer, he's in intensive care I continued,, " Ohh , thank god for that, I was fearing the worst" ah yes" I said sadly, his wife was also in the car", please don't tell me, she had so much to look forward to , with the baby and everything," what", I said aloud," she was pregnant" I said surprisingly, "yes, about three months, she only told me yesterday", Dawn continued," perhaps they were celebrating , everything seemed to be going so well for them".

I went into Dawns bedroom and sat on the bed, "Dawn" I said, my eyes filling with tears, "we got to get someone to listen to us, we've got to stop this before one of us is next".
Dawn sat on the bed next to me and put her hand on my knee, her hand felt cold, even though her room was warm, "I'll have a think about it while I have a bath, oh, Brian will be home tomorrow", she continued, as she kicked her shoes off and started to undress, I watched as she undressed slowly and provocatively taking her shirt off first then her black trousers then folding them neatly to wear the next day, her underwear was black and silky which was my favourite," will you undo me" she asked," of course",

I eagerly replied, my excitement obviously noticeable in my jeans and I met her face to face and in one movement put my hand behind her back and undid her bra," wow, one handed, your good", she whispered, we both smiled, I looked out the window, the sun was shining, no chance of being stopped this time I thought.

Dawn started nibbling my ear as she lowered her arms so her bra just fell, her hands reached my belt, with one hand rubbing the firmness of my crotch and the other undoing my belt, I whispered," wow, one handed, your good" and the next instant she was undoing my button then my zip.

Dawn smiled, she was in control of us both, she gently pushed me backwards onto the bed, I took off my shirt before lying down, Dawn led down beside me rubbing her thigh against mine, her hand slowly working on my boxers before finally pushing them off at my feet, my hand felt the silkiness of her panties and I slid my hand inside.

My hand was working at the silk until I could push no further, she slowly changed positions so I could push her soft silky panties off at her feet too.

Our hands working at our bodies, my hand found her inner thigh and began to move higher until my finger tips found her moist flesh, I parted her and heard a moan, she was enjoying it, probably the last time this happened was months ago, she moved and sat astride me, my eyes met hers and we both smiled, we knew this was so wrong, but so right.

Her body started to move in rhythmic motions, round and round then backwards and forwards, I tried to resist as I didn't want it to end to quick, my hands around her buttocks trying to pull her further onto my throbbing manhood, then I felt it, " Its coming I said, its coming ","yes", Dawn shouted too, but I was to wrapped up in my own ecstasy to understand what she said, we stopped" there's something special about coming together" Dawn said," wow, that was fantastic, that must be the yoga sessions, I said, " but" our minds drifted back to reality at the same time, Dawn read my mind, " so what's our plan then with these bloody puddle people she said.

"Well", Dawn said, "I have some theory's", " go on " I said intrigued, I could feel my manhood getting smaller but Dawn was happy to stay as she was, " well we have not heard of ships or boats just jumping

out of the water or crashing"" no, that's true " I said
,Dawn continued, " well could it be something to do
with the water, but not salt water".
"If we covered the puddles with salt, we could kill off
the puddle people", she said enthusiastically.

"Theory sounds good, but what questions are going
to be asked when we start sprinkling tonnes of salt
all over the place," "ah, " she said, " that's where the
theory starts to collapse".

Reality came upon us both at the same time, as we
both looked at her alarm clock , Dawn quickly went
to her on suite bathroom and went to the family
bathroom, we came out at the same time and went
downstairs, we got to the front door and I said " how
about if I get the water analysed", "ok, I will try and
see if there is a way to dry up all the puddles," ok,
let's do it", we said, as I stepped out the door I said,
same time tomorrow, yes, Dawn said, " I would like
that", I was only joking but I'm sure Dawn was
serious".

I walked across the road to my house and got out
Toms microscope he had for Christmas two years
earlier and found slides and bits and pieces I needed.

Michelle came home first and asked what I was up to ,"I m just looking at water", I said, "nice" she said sarcastically and went into the kitchen, Toni and Tom came in a few minutes later with tales of David's accident.

I was annoyed such crap was going round already, 'she was drunk' 'she driving too fast', 'he was touching her up', the only person to know for sure was lying in a hospital bed, I told them both to go to their rooms, I didn't want to hear it.

I called the hospital and said I was a family member of the Hurst family, the nurse said David was coming round, I said I will finish my tea and come straight down, I hung up, started and finished my tea in about ten minutes then as I put the plate and cutlery in the dishwasher I gave Michelle a kiss, grabbed my mobile from the worktop, keys from the hall table and headed out the door.

As I left the drive I called Dawn to tell her I was going to the hospital, " I'm on my way too" she said, it was too late to tell her no, it was a bad move for both of us, while driving one handed and talking over the phone , trying to avoid the puddles , we both knew how dangerous it would be in the rain, but she cared for me and wanted to know the truth about the accident from David.

I got to the hospital first, wow, there were blue lights and sirens everywhere, there must have been ten police cars and about seven or eight ambulances, the whole scene looked like something out of a movie, that couldn't be a car crash if the puddle people had caused another one ,could it.?

 I turned into the car park to find the fire brigade was there too, ladders going up to the hospital wards, with people being carried down, then stretchers coming down with people on them, some completely covered.

I stood with the onlookers, the emergency services walking right by us but too busy to stop and talk, Dawn caught up with me and we heard the voices and then the laughter from the puddle people, we saw dead bodies, three, four, five six, we counted and then I saw a head, a familiar head, it was David, Dawn spoke to the medic,, " is he ? " she questioned, the medic bowed his head and whispered" yes"," how the hell did they get him inside a hospital,, there are no puddles inside a hospital", I reasoned, I couldn't get my head round it," how the hell did he die then", I said aloud, an onlooker gave me an answer.

" By all accounts", he started, "the bus was coming down the hill, slid on some black ice and crashed through the corner of the intensive care unit, which buckled the drain pipe and sprayed water all over the equipment electrocuting the patients"," you idiot you don't get ice in august.!

" Just saying what I hear," he said, I said sorry and walked away,, I cried out, "Arghh, " and started kicking and jumping up and down in the middle of the puddles," I'll kill you" " I'll kill you all", Dawn was not impressed with my outburst and wondered if I was losing it, reassuringly she asked if I wanted to go back to her place ,I agreed it was a good idea.
I did feel like I was using her, just for a repeat of what happened a few hours earlier, she must have known, as she put her arm around my waist with a squeeze and said " It'll be alright" as we walked back to our cars.

We drove home very carefully and as I led the way I could see the headlights on Dawns Audi swerving to avoid the puddles.

When I got home asked I Michelle if it was ok to keep Dawn company for an hour, Michelle said " that's ok, just don't be late", Michelle suspected nothing and trusted in me, "David died today in a bizarre accident, I'll tell you about it later"..I said.

I walked across the road to Dawns and let myself in, the babysitter had just gone and Brian was just on his way to bed, "goodnight" I said and gave him a high five ,I walked into Dawns lounge and tried to relax on her sofa, it was difficult with so many things going around in my head, but it was made easier when Dawn walked back in wearing just her dressing gown and as she sat down on my lap asked the question, " so what the bloody hell are we going to do".

"I'll have another look at the water sample later," ok" Dawn said with a sigh, "I'll see what I can dig up".

I played with the belt on dawns dressing gown and slowly pulled it loose, " I think we ought to do more work and less play" Dawn said, retying her belt, I knew she was right, but I just didn't like it.

I got up to go, Dawn got up, untying her belt,""you could be right" she said ",it could take our minds off the terrible situation we are in with the puddle people".

"No, you were right I'll go and have a look at the slide with the water on it, it's in the lounge, although I expect Michelle may have thrown it out by now".

I turned and looked at Dawn just before I walked for the door, she was just standing in the middle of the lounge, her gown wide open showing off her soft round breasts, her nipples erect, big enough to hang your coat on and her neat little bush perfectly cut, so very tempting, but we need to be rational, though I must admit I was struggling with it.

I went home, Michelle was watching Pierce Brosnan again I think, I crossed the lounge and sat at the table with the microscope in front of me and the slide still in place, I changed the lens to maximum zoom and looked at the slide, strange, no water just red dust, I took the slide out, no water, "you haven't touched this stuff have you" I asked," nothing to do with me" Michelle replied, the water must have evaporated, but what was the dust.?

It was nearly bedtime and I spent the remaining time looking at the computer screen, I couldn't find anything about red dust apart from references made to the planet mars, it didn't make sense, I sent a text to Dawn with what I found out and said I would see her tomorrow after work, after calling in at the lab on the industrial estate.

The next day was far from normal, with the whole of the office whole staff wearing black armbands, I was in charge now, but I could do without the responsibility at this moment.
But that didn't stop me thinking about other things like the lab results, I needed to know, I really needed to know, I just couldn't concentrate.

I finished work at one pm and took a box full of paperwork home, I got home and dumped the box of paperwork on the table in the hall and with a hard kick, shut the front door ,for Christ's sake, I feel so stressed, right on cue I heard the faint sound of a diesel engine outside, it was Dawn, I opened the door and shouted to her to put the kettle on as she walked up her path ,"ok, " she replied, I gave it two minutes then went across.

Dawn was reading her mail, "ah, this ones from Barry" she said, keen to open it ,he's coming home early and should be home within two weeks" that's fantastic Brian will be looking forward to that" , I said ,though I must admit to being as jealous as hell.

"So, what did the lab say " Dawn asked," well not a lot really, they were still testing the sample and going through their files, they are going to text me later" I said," but the weather forecast is good and it's not going to rain for a few days, allegedly, so we have a little time".

" By the way , I was looking on the net for accidents in our area and there seems to be more here than any other part of the country" Dawn said.

"Anyway, I have to go, I'm in charge now so I have more paperwork to do", again, Dawn made it hard for me to go , "Michelle's not home for ages yet and the kids have after school club", Dawn said as she unbuttoned the top of her shirt, I started to walk away, but just got to the bottom of her stairs, damn it, I thought, I just couldn't resist.

" Well, come on then" I said, she ran towards me and gave me a hug, Dawn seems to be thankful of my love and love making and I was trying to think how could Barry keep going away and leaving this woman behind, so sexy , so irresistible, we made love twice and I felt exhausted, I could have gone to sleep, but heard my mobile play (colonel bogey) the tune for a text message.

Dawn eventually let me get to my phone, the message was from the lab," you're so horny" Dawn said and pushed the duvet away, exposing her naked body, she opened her legs, inviting me in, I turned back to the message.

"It's the lab," I said excitedly, I looked back at dawn, damn, the lab will have to wait, it's not going to rain for a while yet.

we made love again and I could feel my whole body aching all over," not done it three times in a row for a long time ," I said, " how come you stay hard for so long, Dawn asked," it's because you're so damn sexy" I replied with a smile and I think I'm falling in love with you". I continued.

" I've loved you from a distance for a long time" Dawn added.
"lab", I said to break up the seriousness.

I picked up my phone again and started to read the message, a quick look and I told Dawn "they want to know where I got it from as it's the same type of dust that's found in the soil around homey airport, where the hell is homey airport".

"Barry's been there ,before he went to Afghanistan, it's in America, a place beginning with 'n' I think, but ' can't remember", Dawn said knowingly.

We both got dressed and I kissed her on the lips as I left the comfort of her house, I felt very content being in Dawns arms and wanted more, but the puddle people had to be sorted as a priority as we were expecting rain in a few days and I needed to find out about homey airport.

I was sat at the table with paperwork everywhere when the kids came in, followed by Michelle who had picked them up," ah, Tom, your good at geography, have you heard of homey airport" I asked, " yep, it's in America, Niagra, no, Nevada, yeh Nevada, he said, "cheers" I said, "without asking why, he turned and went to his room to change from his school clothes, Toni shouted down from her room," its near groom lake, where all the top secret alien stuff is", she shouted" then added " it's called area 51"again, I shouted back with "cheers".

"What are you working on dear" Michelle asked," oh, it's a client at work, something David was working on, " I hated lying to Michelle and using David's name but it was out of necessity, but my relationship with Dawn was getting stronger and for some reason I didn't feel so guilty, It'll be different when Barry gets back I'm sure.

So how did the water or dust get from area 51 in America to our sleepy little village here in the UK.? could it be carried in the clouds, the wind could have blown it across, or even its been secretly dumped here by the Americans, by planes high in the sky, so many theories, but why the hell here.?

I went to get up from the table to get a glass of wine from the fridge, I could hardly move, I was aching all over, I moaned in the process and Michelle asked if I was ok," yeh, I'm fine, just been sat down to long" it made me think, I really ought to stop these liaisons with Dawn, but at the time it feels so good.

 Another uneventful night, but I spent most of it looking at the internet trying to find out as much as I could about area 51, so many theories, even linked to aliens, how stupid was that.?

The next day in the office I tried to contact someone, or anyone from area 51, needless to say the emails kept bouncing back, it was about five to five and I was looking forward to going home after a long and full day when I had a call from the minister of foreign affairs.

As a company we are trying to break into the American market so I took the call, hoping the minister may be able to help me get a leg up after David's death.

The minister was quite abrupt in his tone, basically saying I am not, under any circumstances to email or try to make contact with anyone from the homey airport, groom lake area, adding it is of national importance and security, I tried getting a word in to explain of the water and red dust and the puddle people but he wasn't having any of it, ending the conversation with," do I make myself clear", " of course, perfectly clear " I said, rather annoyed and then the minister hung up.

I put the phone down slowly, I was in shock, are we just going to let people die at the hands of the puddle people?

I wanted to call back, but the screen on my phone showed the number as ' withheld ' and thought it may be better to let things lie for a while and try to follow more discreet lines of enquiry, but how.? what's Dawn going to say when I see her next.? So many unanswered questions.

I walked out the office filled with worry, but a part of me wanted revenge, but I didn't know if it was for the puddle people or the home office or both, how dare they tell me what to do.
When I got home I had tea then went out to clean the car, I connected the hose and put the brush on the end but my heart wasn't in it, I still felt annoyed, almost angry at the events of the day, I wanted to be with Dawn, she had a calming effect on me, it was wrong, I know, I turned back to wash the car but I didn't want to turn the water on, I felt scared, so I packed the hose and brush away and thought , I'll leave it until I'm a bit more enthusiastic.

" It won't clean itself" Michelle shouted from the kitchen," I'm not in the mood" I shouted back.

Dawn caught my eye, I put my hand up and she motioned me to go and see her.

"Barry Skyped me today and he's coming home a week tomorrow" , "that's great" I said, lying through my teeth, "you look pale or you ok"?, she asked " yes, I had some bad news today, what are you doing tomorrow morning" ,I asked "wow, you are so horny", Dawn said in a whisper," I meant I need to talk to you about the puddle people" Dawns face dropped.
"I'll pop in after Michelle's gone to work, ok", I said , trying to cheer her up," "I suppose it'll have to do" she said, I kissed her on the cheek and left.

The next morning after the kids and Michelle had left, I gathered some paperwork together and was just about to leave for Dawns when the phone rang, it was sergeant Ford from the police station, "good morning sir, this is sergeant Ford from the police station", he began, "are you going to be in this morning"," I'm not sure yet," why do you ask," we would like to ask you some questions, if you don't mind" he said," what sort of questions "I asked," does it matter", he said" no I guess not" I replied," eleven o'clock ok with you" he asked "yes, I'll be here" and the sergeant very rudely put the phone down.

My first thoughts were ' what the hell does he want'.

In a week's time Barry comes home, so no more secret liaison's with Dawn ,still, in a few more weeks he'll be going away again, unless of course Dawn meant what she said and get him to stay home for good this time.

I felt disappointed that Dawn didn't want me more, not just for great sex, but then I am still married, so I have to be the dutiful husband to Michelle.

I tapped gently on Dawns door and went in, she was sat at the dining room table having coffee, I dropped the paperwork on the table next to her cup, "there, we should be able to fight the bastards with that", I said.

"It's going to rain next week" Dawn said with tears in her eyes," I'll be here for you" I said reassuringly.

Dawn picked up some of the papers and started looking at the data," it doesn't make sense to me " she said," well, if you have a look at what the dust is made from and where it comes from that should give you a bit of a clue".

Dawn scanned it quickly," so the puddle people are from area 51 in Nevada or from mars and could be alien," she said sarcastically.

" Sounds like a sc-fi movie to be, it's a bit farfetched she added," the data is there" I said" but how can we get rid of the dust, which effectively are the puddle people. "Dawn asked.
" Ah, that's the awkward bit, we have so many options, we could try and dry up all the puddles and clear the dust within them, we could put something in the puddles if we knew what kills them, we could try spreading salt everywhere, because this is not happening at sea" " it's not happening anywhere else but our village " Dawn moaned.

"Well, its quarter to ten now, I have to see sergeant Ford at my place at eleven" I said," what does he want" Dawn asked," not got a clue, he's a bloody pain in the neck, anyway, we've got to think what we are going to do" I replied.

"The weather is still good, let's see what happens Dawn said, "ok I agreed, but just take care."

" It's nice to see you care " I said as Dawn came up to me.

My heart was beating faster in anticipation of what was coming next, I felt an erection coming on and she hadn't even touched me yet, I wanted to throw the paperwork and coffee cups off the table and take her there and then.

Dawn held on to my collar and took two steps back, so her bottom was against the table edge, she pulled me closer and we started to kiss, wow, that felt so good, with my two hands around her waist I lifted her sweatshirt up and off in one go," red underwear, I like red" I said, Dawn moved to the side and started to undo the buttons of my shirt with one hand while gently caressing my backside with the other, slowly, teasing me.

My hands were desperately trying to undo her bra, it was front fastening, something I wasn't used to, I pulled at the underneath and slid it gently over her breasts then up over her head and arms, I buried my head in her chest, kissing her, feeling each breast soft against my cheeks and rubbing her nipples between my thumb and forefinger until they were erect, her hand gently moving my arms so my unbuttoned shirt would fall to the ground, more and more passion was taking us over, I moved her round so she was now led on the table, I undone the button and zip of her jeans and pulled them and her knickers off in one go, she looked fantastic, I quickly undone my own button and zip then pushed my own jeans and boxers to the floor and stepped out of them, I bent down and kissed her navel, Dawn was led on the table, her long blonde hair falling carelessly over the sides, I put my hands under her back and gently pulled towards me, she pulled me closer, I stopped, just to tease her before entering her, Dawn pulled me in, wow, so warm, her hands slid down my back and as the rhythm intensified, Dawns nails started to dig in to my bare flesh, I screamed out, but found more, I was pushing harder and moving faster, then.., the end!, I held Dawn tight, my legs aching so much, I didn't want to let go in case I slipped to the floor, it must have been two minutes before I slowly released my hold, my heart still beating fast but beginning to settle, I felt I was ready to go again, I pulled out and pulled Dawn off the table, she was looking straight at me with a smile, I turned her round so she was bent over the table then entered her from behind, I don't know where I found the strength or stamina, with Michelle it was once just now and again, I kept going, holding Dawns hips and pulling her harder onto me, then..., the end!, I could go no further after the second time and felt myself exhausted and leaning forward onto Dawns bare back.

I felt tired and could have done with a sleep but we both had things to do, as we got dressed, we both agreed how good sex was, then agreed we should really be sorting other things out.

 As Dawn put the kettle on there was a knock at the door, when Dawn answered, she called back," it's for you" puzzled I went out to the front door to find sergeant Ford standing there, it was eleven o'clock already and I had forgotten, more to the point, how the hell did he know I was here.?

"I'll be right with you, " I'll leave the papers with you Dawn" I said, patted her bum and left with the sergeant.

When we got to my house I was asked more questions, but this time about my emails and attempted phone calls to area 51," I think it's better to just let it go whatever your trying to find" he said, "you don't understand" I pleaded, but it fell on deaf ears, he told me off, and warned me, I guess that what his superiors told him to do.

I saw sergeant Ford to the door and he left without saying another word.

I was annoyed, but at that moment I was more concerned with the stinging from the scratches down my back, I went to the bedroom, but trying to see your back when you have just one mirror was a problem to say the least, I put on a sweatshirt and ran back to Dawns," umm, could you wash my shirt for me, I seem to have got a bit of blood on it "I said," wow, sorry I didn't know we got so intense, yes, I'll wash it now", dawn said, " hell Dawn, I don't know how I'll explain this to Michelle" I said worried," I think you done it on the bonnet of Michelle's car when you were cleaning the engine bay, the underside of the bonnet can have some sharp edges" Dawn said with a smile.

" Anyway, what did sergeant Ford say" Dawn asked, " well, he politely told me to lay off with the phone calls and emails to area 51, this is beginning to be much bigger than we thought", I said.

We both scanned the internet and local paper for any more accidents over the past two weeks, we found nothing to link any accidents to the puddle people. "something just isn't right" I said.

I left Dawns house and went back to work with thoughts of Dawn, Michelle, area 51 and work related sales on my mind all at the same time, I just couldn't concentrate, when I finally got home around six pm, Michelle said I looked pale and should take some time off, I agreed as soon as work settles down a bit, you always think your bosses job is easy until you have to do it yourself, that was certainly the case with David's job.

An uneventful night, except I went to bed later than Michelle so she couldn't see the marks on my back, I also got up a little later so she had already gone downstairs.
I watched the weather forecast on TV, possible showers with a sunny outlook, what the hell do we make of that, is it going to rain or not.?
I felt that I really needed to know.

After a rather boring day, I again finished work around six, I stepped outside the office to see black clouds, I actually ran home for fear of getting caught in the rain and as I got to the front door it started to hail, I stepped in and promptly said" ha, you bastards didn't get me this time"" Tony," Michelle shouted" sorry" I said," I take it you mean the hailstones" yes of course" I replied, I actually meant the puddle people.

" Dawn said Barry will be home at the end of the week" Michelle said" I didn't think he was due home for another couple of weeks" I said, pretending not to know, I didn't go into the kitchen where Michelle was straight away, as I didn't like to be face to face when I was deceiving her.

I sat down at the computer to find out more about the soil at area 51.
 After spending more than an hour and a half I got nowhere, all the computer really told me was the Nevada desert was sandy and we knew that already.

I remember sometime in the past and every now and again there has been some sort of red dust or sand on cars, rooftops and just about everywhere and we are told its the sand in the rain that comes from the Sahara, I wonder who put that rumour around !, how about if it was from the Nevada desert, would anybody know? and if from Nevada could it be from around the homey airport, groom lake area, I mean, could it be from area 51.

Could the Americans be dumping their sand stuff ,
contaminated soil or whatever on our sleepy little
village, someone must know, because I have been
warned off by sergeant Ford and from the minister,
what's more, I don't want to " just let it go " as he
says.

What people like the dopey sergeant Ford doesn't
know is that in 1988 a Russian spy satellite photo,
apparently shows that large amounts of soil had
been recently removed from an area just north of
the project 57 contaminated zone, which is in area
13 and a water well drilled for dust suppression so
that the plutonium dust didn't go up into the
atmosphere.

Project 57 by the way was the first of many safety
experiments which was the test series for operation
Plumbob, in 1957.!

The project 57 site was added to the Nevada test site
and called area 13, area 13 is said to be north of
groom lake.

so what I have been thinking is, if the Americans
started testing nuclear explosions and plutonium and
all those sorts of things in 1957, is it possible that the

soil which was contaminated was taken away and dumped somewhere, which is what the Russian spy satellite saw removed in 1988.!

Wow, that's a 41 year difference ,that's a lot of soil.

Then it is possible that for 41 years ,the earth has been contaminated.

I wonder what happens to the soil if you add water to it, does it take on a new life of its own and would it make any strange sounds.? ,of course it wouldn't, would it.?
I think I need to do more research before I jump up and down accusing anyone, most of all, a world super power.

What's with all this alien stuff at area 51, well I'm a none believer so I reserve judgement there.
If there were such things as aliens and they are normally seen around Nevada could they somehow be involved in this dust, rain, puddle people voices thing.?

But why our village.?

I looked up, wow, I had got completely carried away with all this, it was now showing ten pm, I had done the paperwork but nothing else, I couldn't even remember what we had for tea.

Michelle was just drying her hair, how come you've dyed it blonde " I asked," just fancied a change, do you like it" she asked " yep, looks good" I said, I thought of how much she now looked like Dawn and remembered the kitchen table.

Both of us went to bed around half ten, with Dawn playing on my mind while I was in bed, Michelle noticed I was aroused and cuddled in to me, at first my thoughts were,' oh my god, not again', but I had to make it look good, so I gave her a kiss and, as it turned out she was almost asleep, for the first time in my life I was glad not to make love.

The next morning I woke with the puddle people on my mind, I found a link, Dawn had said Barry had been to Nevada and we had the fine dusty sand soil stuff over here in the same village as he lives, maybe a coincidence or was I slowly getting jealous and wanted someone to blame for the accidents.

Barry comes home in a couple of days, so it may be worth having a quiet word in his ear,
we all had breakfast and was about to leave for work when Michelle came back in from the drive and said the car won't start, I went out and tried but the battery seemed completely dead, "ok, I'll put it on charge before I go to work ", I said, Michelle called the kids who were not best pleased at having to walk to school and I walked towards the garage to get the battery charger, after connecting up the charger I got my paperwork together and went to work.

Really busy day from the start, with so many emails and most of them relating to the weather, I guess the sites I have been going on must have been using cookies, the bad weather was coming tonight the reports said, brilliant, I thought, now what's going to happen, I just wanted the deaths to stop.

I called Dawn from work and as I did ,the ringing tone from her phone changed, which made it seem like she was abroad," hello dear, where are you" I asked, Dawn answered in a very chirpy," I'm down at the old chapel, yoga classes today" oh, yes" I replied, "the ringing tone sounded like you were abroad,"" I wish", Dawn answered," do you know anyone with a new black ford galaxy with blacked out windows" I asked " nope, why what's up" I think Dawn could hear the concern in my voice, "hello Dawn, hello , talk to me, I can't hear you", the phone went dead, 'I looked back and the black ford was still following me from a distance, I was starting to get nervous.

If someone was trying to get to me they were doing a good job of it.

 When I got home I went straight upstairs and looked out through the blinds in Toms bedroom window, the black ford galaxy drove slowly past, I think it's the same one as got me soaked the other day.

Michelle was in the kitchen preparing tea and the kids were at after school club," I'm just going to check the battery on the car and pop over and see Dawn a minute" I said," ok, don't be long, tea will be ready in about twenty minutes" Michelle replied.

I tapped on the door and went in, Dawn was getting Brian's tea," do you want to have tea in your room Brian" Dawn asked " yes please" Brian answered and as soon Brian had gone upstairs Dawn said " what's up", I told Dawn about the black ford galaxy and then being followed, then the phone signal," oh, I thought you hung up on me" she said," nope, I think we were cut off"," well I had a text earlier I think it was from Barry saying he loved me and he is desperate to tell me something about what he saw in America, he signed off as Barry but no number was visible, who do you think it could have been " asked Dawn" do you remember when sergeant Ford came round the other day, how did he know I was here" ,I said.

This puddle people problem is bigger than we ever thought," can we go to the press", Dawn asked " and say what, that we keep hearing voices", I said.

We stood looking at each other for a minute, searching for the answer" oh, any chance of taking me down to royals garage when you have a minute please, "I asked, " of course, anything for you , anything else I can do."? Dawn smiled" have we got time for anything else" I asked," well the garage is shut and Brian is upstairs so I guess the answer is no then" Dawn said," well my tea is just about ready so that's two no's then", I said.

I went back home and told Michelle we needed a new battery and had asked Dawn if she would drive one of us to the garage tomorrow, I had tea with Michelle and sat down to watch top gear, Michelle had vacated to the kitchen after tea to watch coronation street although I can't see why anybody would want to watch as they are always arguing , there's no happiness, anyway, the next thing I knew it was just gone ten and the kids were coming home. "Wow, you ought to see the accident outside the chapel", shouted Tom as he got in," a truck with no driver ploughed straight into a car like mums", my first words were, "has it been raining"? " no its just starting to " he said.

"I wonder if this storm will affect Barry coming home tomorrow" I said, for some reason I felt rather smug that he'll be caught up in the storm, "not sure, but I'm thinking more of how lucky we were to have had a flat battery, or we would have been parked in the same place " Michelle said "yes, very lucky, very lucky indeed "I said.

 I wondered if the powers that be were trying to kill us or scare us, they can't be, can they.? I phoned Dawn and asked what time she was going to pick up Barry tomorrow, she said just after school , but she was due to take Brian back to the hospital for checks after his fall, so I asked Dawn if Michelle could borrow her car to pop down to the garage after school tomorrow, Dawn said "yes of course, if Michelle could drop us off at the hospital then pick

Barry up that would be great", "ok, I could come and pick you both up after I've put the new battery on", the deal ended with Barry being able to shower, change and be ready to surprise Brian when we all got home.

Why do you keep asking if it's going to rain" Michelle asked, " I'm just a bit fed up with all the rain we keep having, it's a shame we couldn't live in a warm country,"" what are you talking about, it's been fine for a few days, we only had a bit of a shower " Michelle said," yep, perhaps your right " I agreed with a sigh.

We had pizza delivered even though we had eaten earlier and went to bed stuffed full, I looked out of the window just before getting into bed and wondered if we were going to be disturbed during the night as it was raining harder now, I led awake for about twenty minutes with Michelle cuddling into me, wow, it felt just like Dawn, though not so energetic.

The alarm went off as normal the next morning, Toni must have been awake and heard it," for Christ sake, when is this bloody rain going to stop," Toni moaned, "it's been raining all night" I said, thinking how many big puddles there are going to be.

"What time are you working till" Michelle asked," don't know yet, trying to see how things pan out with Barry coming home", I said ,without really caring," I think when you finish work if you use Dawns car and come and pick me up, we could go and get the new battery, come back and while I fit it, according to how time is going you could go to get Barry."

" Sounds like half a plan" Michelle said," I'll go across and run it past Dawn to see if it's ok" she added" ok, I'm off to work in a few minutes, I'll see you after work, about three" I said, Michelle gave me a kiss and I headed for the door, shouting to the kids as she went," see you later dad" Toni and Tom said together," wait, what time are you two back this evening", I shouted," bout six" Toni shouted back, I then shut the lounge door and was ready to go to work.

Watching the weather forecast on the TV it said rain and strong winds were likely this afternoon, I hadn't realized it had stopped raining in the last ten minutes.

I feared the worst and thought about putting off the trip to the garage and telling Michelle not to go to the station to meet Barry, but that would have been pointless as she probably wouldn't have listened anyway.

I was ready for work, so let's see what the office has in store for me today, as soon as I walked outside the front door, it started, the voices, the laughter, I shouted at them," who are you going to kill today, come on, bring it on", I kicked the puddles as I walked to work, waiting for them to trip me up.

As I got to the front door of the office I shouted again," didn't get me this time you cowards".

The day dragged, from start to finish, till Michelle picked me up at three, Michelle pulled up in Dawns car right outside the front door, she had stopped in a puddle and as I got to the car I gestured to her to move forward," what are you frightened to get your feet wet" she laughed, but moved forward anyway, I got in expecting something to happen, but nothing did.

"First stop royals garage driver please", I said" I suppose a new battery is going to cost seventy quid" Michelle said, as we got underway, "oh, would you mind not driving in the puddles, I told Dawn we would try and keep the car clean so it looks like it's been cared for when you pick up Barry," Michelle made some sarcastic comment but I was nervous of the puddles to pay any real attention.

We got to royals garage unscathed and Michelle was right, the new battery did cost seventy quid, " next stop home please driver" I said"," yes sir" Dawn said laughing, we got home and Michelle turned straight round and went to pickup Barry," should be back about five" she said as she drove away, I looked at my watch, it was twenty past three, after I replaced the car battery I went across to Dawns to see if they were ready to go to the hospital," yep, ready when you are" Dawn said" you ready Brian" I said and Brian nodded his head.

We walked back across the road, avoiding the puddles, with Dawn and myself looking up at more black clouds, do you think Michelle's going to be alright in my car" Dawn asked nervously, worried that is was going to continue raining, "I'm sure she'll be fine," I said, unconvincingly," I'll call her in a while" I continued.

I called Michelle's mobile and she answered it, that's all I needed to know, but I asked if she was ok," I think my next car is going to be an Audi convertible this car is fantastic" she said " ok, as long as you're ok," I said and blew her a kiss down the phone. We got to hospital and the hailstones started, "phew, that was close." Dawn said, " yes, did you hear the laughter", I said," yes, let's get in quick" Dawn said.

We made our way to the children's ward where Brian was going to be checked over, Dawn gave the receptionist Brian's full name and the receptionist apologised as the doctor was running about twenty minutes behind.

" Well I think it's safe to say Barry will be home before Brian now ", I whispered.

We had been waiting about fifteen minutes when all hell broke loose throughout the whole hospital, with bells, sirens, buzzers and flashing lights everywhere, we looked around in amazement as many of the staff were running to do an emergency job of some sort.

" Excuse me, could you tell us what's happening" I asked, " I'm sorry sir, we have an emergency coming in" a nurse told us, we waited a few more minutes and decided to ring Michelle to tell her we were further delayed," damn, no network coverage" I said to Dawn," try in a couple of minutes, it might be atmospherics due to the storm" Dawn reassuringly said.

We heard the doctor say he was sending two extra nurses down to emergency to cope with the extra work, " wow, something bad has happened" I said aloud," a bomb has gone off under a car transporter", one of the other patients said," shit, it can't be the puddle people this time" Dawn whispered," "yes, perhaps your right, but we have a bit longer to wait now" I moaned.

" I think it was an Audi" one of the other patients" said, I spun round on my seat," what was", I asked, then the lady patient told me it was an Audi with a soft roof that was under the car transporter when it blew up.

I tried ringing Michelle again and got through this time, the phone rang, but went to answer phone, I left a message to call me as soon as possible.

I was distraught, but Dawn was calm, though her eyes were filled with tears," "Dawn, how far do you think it is to the station" I asked fearing the worst, " it's about three miles but don't be so silly, you don't even know where the accident has happened, it could be anywhere"" yes. yes, sorry, I wasn't thinking", I said tearfully.

I tried ringing again but still no answer," come on, we got to get down to emergency" I said.

trying not to run but hurry and find the accident and emergency department was stressful to say the least when there are so many corridors and so few signs, it seemed to take forever, but we found it, there were four stretchers with nurses next to them by the main doors, we heard the ambulances then saw the blue lights get closer, then the doctors opened the doors and the nurses rushed out to meet the medics, they came back in, slower ,one, two, three, four, four bodies then the doors closed, Barry and Michelle were not   amongst them, we both looked at each other wondering what the hell to do next. I ran outside to the first ambulance and asked if there was anybody else," just two more sir, that's all we can say" "are they in the car,? is it an Audi ?" I was running along with the ambulance as it started to move off, Dawn pulled me back, " look there's another one coming" she said, " yes, but it's not flashing" I replied, the three of us froze, fearing the worst, although Brian didn't really understand much of it.

The ambulance crew wheeled the bodies in past us " stop" I shouted, there was a name tag turned upside down on each of the covered bodies, I had never seen that before, I questioned the driver why it had been done and he said " it was done at the scene by a plain clothed officer, American I think" both Dawn and myself quickly turned the tags over, it was Barry and Michelle we were certain, but it was not their names on the tags,, it was ours.!

" oh, my god" we said both together, Dawn immediately broke down in tears, with Brian crying too, I was more annoyed than emotional at that moment, the police must have thought that because Barry and Michelle were in the Audi, they were us.

" Those bastards, they done this" I looked at Dawn and Brian, they were both in floods of tears and sobbing uncontrollably, one of the nurses gently pushed me to one side and the ambulance crew pushed the bodies along the corridor, a doctor stopped us as we were about to follow into a side ward.

" Excuse me, you are" he questioned, Dawn told him our names and the doctor seemed shocked, hardly surprising really, as he thought we were lying on a stretcher," have you any I.D." he asked," listen you bloody idiot, my wife and this ladies husband have just died and your asking us for I,D." I was getting more angry by the second, two burly security guards stepped forward," don't, or I'll ripping your f*^"**g heads off", the security men stopped and the doctor gestured for them to leave us.

"I'm doctor Hughes, there seems to be some sort of mix up with the names", "really, why would you think that ", Dawn said through her tears, "here we can use this office" the doctor said and held out his arm to show us the office.

After being settled we began to regain our composure.

" It is obvious you know the deceased, you are the husband and wife, yes" he asked and I went through the story of why the two of them were together and the two of us together," Have you any idea why they would have your name tags on the bodies" , " yes, because the people who killed them thought they were us and the tags were put on by the Americans who are frightened by the two of us," Dawn said , "that's a pretty strong allegation, would you like to share your reasoning behind it", the doctor asked, I put my hand on Dawns shoulder and shook my head," no, it doesn't matter anymore" she said.

A medic knocked on the door, then came in and gave the doctor some paperwork, " I can see how the mix up occurred" he said," there was no mix up, they thought it was us" Dawn said" but what happened" she continued.

"Well it seems there was a huge explosion under a car transporter, probably the fuel tank and it rocked the transporter so bad that one of the cars on the top fell off at the exact moment the Audi was going past and due to the car being a convertible crushed the car and the occupants inside, wow, the likely hood of that happening must have been a million to one" the doctor said.

" Yes, that's a bloody coincidence," Dawn said sarcastically.

"The police couldn't find any ID. in the car", the doctor added," what do you mean, no I.D. in the car, Michelle had her handbag with her, her driving licence and her mobile phone" I said," yes and Barry would have had his kit bag, paperwork, tag and I.D.".,
Dawn said.
" I'm very sorry, but there was nothing in the car apart from the occupants", the doctor said, needless to say, both Dawn and myself were stunned and very angry, we both looked at each other and began to leave," we will need formal identification the doctor said," we will be back later when I checked with the babysitter" Dawn said, we left the office totally disgusted by the whole affair.

There were so many unanswered questions.
Did the puddle people cause the accident.?
How did the fuel tank, just explode, on the car transporter.?
Were the Americans involved.?
What happened to Michelle and Barry's personal stuff.?
Why was the car on the top of the transporter not secured.?
That's just five questions off the top of my head.

Before we left the hospital I phoned for a taxi, I thought it may be the best thing to do with everything going round in our heads at the moment and feeling so angry, within two minutes a taxi arrived, we were about to get in when Dawn noticed three identical cars, all black , all ford galaxy's with blacked out windows and all starting to drive away at the same time.

I stopped and stood there contemplating what to do ," I've had enough of this shit", I said and ran towards the first car, all three cars stopped and all four doors opened on each car at the same time, twelve men stepped out in combat gear and wearing flak jackets then just stood there, not doing anything, Dawn pulled me back.

Bang, a shot rang out and hit the street camera outside the hospital showering glass on the pavement below ,we stopped and crouched in the road," Jesus, what was that all about", I said, I looked up to see the men in flak jackets had not moved a muscle, they must have known what was going to happen, we heard the revving of a car engine and turned to see the taxi speeding away, we were left there in the middle of the street in a standoff.

We felt a few spots of rain, this is going to be interesting I thought ,I wonder if any of the three fords will have an accident.

With military precision all twelve doors of the three fords shut at the same time , you could just make out the men inside looking straight at us.

All three cars left in the same direction, one behind the other, we watched them as they took the final turn at the bottom of the street.

As though it all been planned, sergeant Ford turned up and asked if we had organized a taxi home," would we be standing here if we had a taxi" Dawn said, angry that everything seem to have been planned," do you want a lift home, it looks like it's going to rain" the sergeant said with a smile," yes, I'm sure Brian would like a lift" Dawn said," stuff your lift, I'm going to walk" I said," but it's nearly three miles" Dawn said," well I'm going into see Michelle anyway" I said as I turned away and started walking towards the hospital, feeling annoyed that the sergeant didn't try and reason with me.

" Are you sure you don't want a lift" Dawn said from the police car" nope, I'm going inside, I'll see you later", I said and the police car drove away, as I walked back towards the hospital I heard crying, strange squeaky crying, again, like the Cadburys smash Martians from the 70's adverts.

I sent a text to Dawn, come back A.S.A.P.

I went back into the hospital for the identification of Michelle's body, I went to the reception and told the lady behind the desk, at that moment I felt composed and in control, but I knew this is going to be a difficult time, but as one of the staff showed me the way to the mortuary I felt like I was falling to pieces, god's sake, I was missing Michelle, but even though I was going to see Michelle, I was also missing Dawn, it felt so wrong and I was left wondering what we are going to do when this settles down.

I identified Michelle, she still looked good and as I looked at her, just lying there, motionless, I could see a little resemblance between her and Dawn, although I think someone moved her hair as to try and hide the nasty bruise and cut on her head, I held her hand, I know she's gone, but I couldn't help talking to her, I simply said...." I love you", and put her hand back on the bed.

I then returned to the waiting room and waited for Dawn, as soon as Dawn walked in I had to ask," did you hear" Dawn jumped in with" the crying, yes I did if that's what you were going to ask"," what do you think" I said, not knowing whether I wanted to hear Dawns answer or not," I think the puddle people killed the wrong couple, Barry and Michelle were supposed to be me and you"," yes I'm aware of that"," but how could the puddle people create an explosion.? I questioned, "maybe they didn't, the Americans done it, think about it, how come the camera was shot and broken just before you were going to confront them" Dawn said.

There were more men than just the ones in the cars.

The doctor came to see Dawn and took her down to identify Barry.
Dawn returned after about fifteen minutes, in floods of tears," we've got to tell somebody, it's not fair, why us.? why Barry.?"Dawn asked, or Michelle I asked, "but how,? you saw this evening how protected the puddle people are, they seem to have half the American army on their side, what we need to ask is why".?

"Barry said he wanted to talk to me about something he saw while he was in America, I think It's something to do with the men in the black cars", Dawn said, "Shhhh, I don't think this is the right place to talk about it, you never know who's watching or listening", I said with a whisper.

What time is your babysitter due to go home tonight" I asked, " oh, I told her we may be late, so she is welcome to stay the night" Dawn said.

" Got it" I said" go on then" asked Dawn," well, bare with me on this one, I think Barry saw something in area 51 while he was there and wanted to tell you, the men in the black ford galaxy's were from the security at area 51 who knew Barry saw something, he needed to be kept quiet so the plan was to kill Barry and you because they didn't know how much Barry had told you, it just happened that because Michelle had dyed her hair the other day they thought Michelle was you, also she was driving your car" I said.

" Well, that does sound about right, the only thing is, why didn't they kill Barry in Afghanistan and say it was a stray bullet.?and sergeant Ford knows we have a close relationship, they will assume I might have told you about whatever it is I'm supposed to know, I worry about you, I've lost my husband, my friend and I don't want to lose my lover too", she said tearfully.
" Thank you for your concern," I said, we both held each other, Dawn felt so good, warm and soft, I didn't want to let go, her soft touch reminded me of the intimate moments we had spent together.

"So what we got to find out is what Barry knew, unless we don't want to know" I said," well I want to know why and how the puddles are killing people" Dawn said," yes, I think I'll go along with that, I think tomorrow or over the next couple of days I'll have a word with sergeant Ford and see what he's got to say for himself" I said.

"I'm going to have a couple of days off, but my main concern is how am I going to tell the kids."? Toms going to go ballistic, he's always been a mummy's boy".

We went back to the car park, got in the car and headed for home, the rain had stopped, but I went the long way home to avoid the big puddle in south street, when we got home I kissed Dawn goodnight and told her I would see her in the morning, "no I'll come with you to tell Toni and Tom", she said.

I think this must be, without a doubt the hardest thing I have ever had to do, Dawn and myself stepped in through the front door," Toni, Tom ,can I have a word" I called," be there in a minute" Tom shouted back, I guess he was on his Xbox," no, now" I demanded.

Toni and Tom came down the stairs reluctantly," I need a word, come and sit down" they both looked at Dawn then back at me, we sat around the table, I felt like crying, but I knew I had to be strong and it felt comforting having Dawn by my side.

A big sigh, then," we've been down the hospital, mum and Barry was involved in a car accident earlier" I could feel my eyes filling with tears, Toni started to cry, as Dawn held my hand, I could sense Dawn was in tears too, without even looking at her.

Tom was looking at me as though he didn't believe me and just didn't want to hear anymore," mum died with Barry in the accident", I said, I could hear and feel the hurt in my own voice, we all sat at the table, all four of us in tears, our hands crossing the table, holding each other.

I composed myself before telling Dawn she was welcome to join us for supper, she agreed, Dawn got up, kissed the kids then me, then left in floods of tears, I held Toni and Tom, my arms didn't seem long enough to go around the two of them properly, I just didn't want to let them go.

Toni regained her composure first," so what happened dad" she asked, I told them both about the explosion, the car transporter and the car being a soft top," remind me never to get a cabriolet ",Toni said," can we go and see mum" tom said, I delicately told them that due to the injuries it would not be a good idea, but told them they could help with the funeral arrangements, more tears, which started me off again too.

After we gained our composure I rang Dawn and told her we were having a pizza delivery in about twenty minutes for supper, if she was up to it, none of us really felt like eating, but we made a point of doing so as we had not eaten for hours.

Dawn and Brian came over just as the pizza man was leaving," ah, perfect timing, come on in" I said.

More questions came from all three kids as Dawn and myself tried to answer them without breaking down.

" There's no need for you to go to school tomorrow" I said to Toni and Tom, Dawn said the same to Brian.

"We'll have to go back down to the hospital tomorrow to see if there's going to be a post mortem," what's a post mortem mum" asked Brian" it's when the doctors check daddy to see why he died", Brian seemed happy enough with the answer and continued eating pizza, I don't think its hit Brian as much as the rest of us, as Barry was always away from home, I wouldn't have thought there would be a post mortem, I expect it to be covered up quickly, " can we sue the car transporter people" Tom asked, it's not as easy as that , mum and Barry were in the wrong place at the wrong time" I replied, Dawn looked at me, but said nothing.

"We have so much to do, telling friends and family, we will need to find a funeral director, a place for a wake and umm" I could fill my eyes filling with tears, once again, Toni could see it and gave me a hug, but burst into tears herself.

" I'll call Michelle's work first thing in the morning, she was part time at the school, but they have a right to know, it would be wrong to find out from a newspaper or from someone else" I said," well, I phoned Barry's commanding officer just before I came out and he already knew, saying as Barry was in the army they had a right to know as a matter of national security, I think the whole thing is a farce, the commanding officer was told by a police sergeant, a man called Ford" Dawn said.

"Hmmm, he's bugging me, I think I'll have a quiet word with him after the funeral , I'm going to ask for Michelle's personal items and see what the score is" I said, we talked until about eleven pm, Dawn kissed the kids and me then picked up Brian and went home and the three of us went to bed.

The next morning we were all tired, none of us had slept hardly, with all three of us hearing each other crying at sometime during the night, my mind drifted to Dawn so I rang her to see if she was ok, she said she never went to bed, just had a few minutes in the chair while looking at old photos of Barry to try and get some clue of what he saw in America.

I went to the airing cupboard to get a clean sweatshirt and saw Michelle's spare work clothes there, what do I do with them I thought, I closed the cupboard door without taking the sweatshirt out, I just couldn't face it, I went into the bedroom and just sat on the bed, I was lost, I felt my life had been ripped apart, I made the decision then to sort the puddle people out as soon as the funeral was over, starting with sergeant Ford, he knows something, I'm sure of it.

Toni came down to breakfast followed by Tom ,"dad, we've been thinking about the music at mums funeral, can we choose it" Toni asked," yes, if that's what you want, we can choose a song each", I said.

" Mine and your mums song was endless love by Diana Ross and Lionel Ritchie" I said with tears in my eyes, I've heard of them", Tom said innocently, it was the first time I had smiled for a few days.

We had cereals for breakfast, I just couldn't be bothered to do boiled eggs or a full English, it just didn't seem to be my job, even though I would have to start doing it.

" I have to go down to the hospital this morning and then into town, what are you two doing" I asked," not sure yet, I have some course work to finish, Toni said, Tom just shrugged his shoulders.

" I don't like to say it but it has always been respect thing to wear black at a funeral", I said , waiting for a response," what do you think mum would have wanted" Tom asked," it's something you never really talk about, have you got anything black apart from your school uniforms, I asked," of course, but it would be nice to wear something new", Toni said, I never realised it until then how much alike Toni and Michelle were, I could feel the tears rolling down my cheeks," that's fine, we'll see if we can find something in town later" I said.

I left the table and went to the bedroom ,I sat on the bed, how long can this hurt go on for.? I questioned, I must have been there for a while, as Dawn called round about half nine and came up to the bedroom and sat on the bed next to me," any chance of a lift, my cars broken" she asked, with a fake smile.

" Of course, we've got to go to the hospital, then the funeral directors then a bit of shopping, so if you want to tag along that's fine by me, we could all help each other" I said,
we got down to the hospital around ten thirty, it was strange going back into the hospital after the night before, I now seem to have an aversion to hospitals, we went to the reception and asked to see someone about getting a death certificate or if there was going to be a post mortem when would it be done," that's all been done", the receptionist said and handed me a large brown envelope, I looked at Dawn and she asked if there was an envelope with her name on it, there was, " that was quick" I said," yes, it was all done last night" the receptionist said.

I whispered to Dawn " something is definitely not right".

we all left the hospital with all the paperwork and with Dawn and me wondering how everything has been done so quick, perhaps we were being sceptical, or maybe that's the way it is, as we have never done this before we just didn't know.

We drove the short way into town with the radio on to keep our minds on something else other than the thoughts of the forthcoming funerals.

The weather followed the news and it said we were in for some warm weather for the next two days followed by a couple days of low pressure," that could mean rain for the funerals" I said," yes, funerals always seem worse in the rain" Dawn said.

Just before we got to town Dawn had a call on her mobile, a withheld number, she answered it cautiously and it was from Barry's commanding officer asking when she has a date for the funeral could she let him know as there was friends at the camp who would like to attend," yes, I will" Dawn said, then put her phone down," it was Barry's c.o. he wants to attend the funeral, I felt like telling him to go to hell," Dawn said.

" It might be an idea to just let it go till the end of the week" I said, " steady, your beginning to sound like sergeant Ford" Dawn said.

" Dad, is it ok to have ' the 12th of never by Donny Osmond", asked Toni," wow, you'll have everybody in tears, but what a great choice, mum loved Donny Osmond", I said, " yes, I thought so, I may not have shown it all the time, but I loved mum too", she continued, in a flood of tears.

" Why has all the songs got to make you cry" Tom asked, "I think it's the lyrics Tom, it just makes you cry because it's a sad moment" I said, not really knowing how to answer.
"Well I've been looking on you tube and there was a boy band in the sixties called the Beatles and they sang a song called Michelle, can I use that one tom asked," of course, I think that's a great song", I said, I started to sing the song, but pulled over to the side of the road, I was crying my heart out," I'm sorry dad", said Tom, I put my hand up in the air as a gesture that it's ok.

Dawn was in the passenger seat and put her hand on my knee, just like Michelle used to do, it made me look through my tears at Dawn, I wanted to say I love you, but I just couldn't with the kids in the car.

We got to the shops and parked the car, "look", Dawn whispered, just across the car park was a black ford galaxy with blacked out windows," my god, I thought that would have been finished now", I said.

Suddenly the cars indicators flashed twice," somebody's getting in it", Dawn said, we watched but the only person coming through the car park was a young woman, we expected four men in combat gear ,the lady turned round and looked directly at us before she got in the car, started it and drove away," my god, how paranoid are we" Dawn said.
We done our shopping and headed for home, happy with our purchases and thinking Michelle would have liked what we chose.

When we got home, Toni and Tom went to their rooms and Dawn and Brian went home, giving us all a hug and a kiss before they went.

We were only home ten minutes and I made the call to the undertakers, lots of heartbreaking questions, and, although I shouldn't think of it, it did seem rather expensive, Michelle and I had talked about what would happen if one of us died and we had always said that we would be cremated, which was the cheaper option, it just happened to work out that way.

Toni and Tom came down the stairs in their new clothes, I nodded my approval as I had just taken another call from a well wisher saying how sorry they were about my sad loss, it seems to me that it might be the wrong way ,but, why can't we put a big advert in the local paper telling people what has happened, it would save so much hassle, but then perhaps thats me sounding off.

The phone went again and I felt like telling the caller to stop bothering me, but it was Dawn and that's the sort of person I do like bothering me," hi babe what can I do for you", I said, trying to be cheerful" well you can start by looking across to the road at the top of the hill, there's been an accident, she said.

" I shouldn't worry too much it's not been raining for a while" ,I said, " I take it you've not looked out the window in the last hour then ?,she questioned, I did and it was pouring with rain, even though the sun was shining," I thought I heard on the radio it was going to nice for a couple of days." I said," yes, with the possibility of showers", Dawn said.

" You must be able to see it quite well from your back garden, can I come over with the binoculars " I asked," don't be silly, you don't need to ask, come on over", Dawn said.

looking at the accident from Dawns back garden you could plainly see an ambulance, which normally means someone's been hurt, or worse, " I'm half tempted to be nosey and go and take a look", I said to Dawn," I don't think there's any need of that, go out the front by the driveway" Dawn said, I was intrigued, so I went out the back garden and along the path towards the driveway, but before I got to the drive I could hear the squeaky laughter, but we're nowhere near the accident and now I can hear the voices too.

" Dawn, what the hell are they saying" I asked, " I don't know, I can't quite get it either" Dawn replied.

 Could be anything " Dawn said" be a love and put the kettle on, I'm getting a bit fed up with it all now", I said, we went into Dawns kitchen," I remember that table, it nearly killed me, oh, that reminds me, have you still got my shirt," I asked with a smile," yes, I'll get it later" Dawn said," I want to sort this after the funeral, I was expecting it all to stop when Barry died, but now someone else has been killed, there's nobody else locally that knew Barry went to area 51 or even America" Dawn moaned," steady, you don't know if anyone's been killed yet," I said," Tony, you're so caring, you've been so wrapped up and worried about other people, you've failed to understand, we can hear voices from the puddles, but when the voices turn to laughter someone dies" Dawn said.

I started thinking while Dawn was pouring the tea," you know, thinking about it, the accidents that have happened and the people who have died, none of them seemed to be linked to Barry or America or anything, except one". I said" who's that then" Dawn asked, "Brian ,if I hadn't done C.P.R. on him he may have gone too", I said, I was left pondering Dawns last statement and decided to confront sergeant Ford after the funeral, I told Dawn and we agreed, no backing down.

It's wrong to say, but we were not bothered about whoever died in the accident, we would get to hear about it soon enough ,our kids were in their in rooms and we were certain they couldn't be hurt.

The day of the funeral came up very quick, it seemed to be an emotional roller coaster this past week, with so many things to organise, even small things like getting the kids dinner and tea, but the day was here and we could finally say our goodbyes, Barry's funeral was also at the crematorium and it just happened it was the one after Michelle's.
We were ready early, Toni and Tom were in their new clothes, their mum would have been so proud, it bought a tear to my eye, the hearse and the funeral car was perfectly on time, apart from a few black clouds it looked like it was going to be a nice day for a funeral,, if that's possible.

There was so many people waiting at the crematorium, many we didn't know, we assumed they were from Michelle's work, it seemed strange that straight after Michelle's would be Barry's and we were going to be there for ages, along with many of our neighbours.

I saw Dawn and she was wearing the little black dress she wore to a couple of weeks ago, she was stunning, Brian also had new clothes, he looked very handsome and grown up holding his mother's hand.

With the normal professionalism everything went fine with Michelle's funeral as did Barry's, even though there was a moment when Dawn met Barry's c.o. , I was expecting Dawn to give him a slap, but Dawn was very composed and lady like, though you could see the frustration , I think our agreement about sorting the problem after today was a good idea.

I think Dawn would been have less composed if she would have seen whose car was parked by the overhanging willow tree in the car park, I recognised the registration and anyway, there are not very many occasions when you see a police car in a crematorium car park.

All we needed now was the three black ford galaxy's and that would upset us both, it was just starting to rain when we said our goodbyes to the last of the family and friends who had came to show their last respects and as we said to all of them to come back to the grand hotel for a gathering, we looked forward to seeing them there.

Many of the friends and relatives came back to the hotel, even though they said they were caught in a traffic jam caused by an accident, both Dawn and myself didn't give it any thought as to who it may have been, we were to wrapped up in meeting people at the hotel, the whole day had gone without a hitch.

We had been at the hotel about three hours and by then nearly all the people had left, Dawn was just starting to help the caterers clear up when Toni whispered to me" the black car you were looking at the other day in town,! there's three of them outside" I thanked her and thought of how grown up she had become.

I went into the lounge bar and looked out the window at the men in combat gear and flak jackets, they seem to be having some sort of argument , hang on, there's only eleven this time, I tried looking in the cars to see the missing one but with the cars blacked out windows it was difficult to see, I went back into the hall and helped the caterers and Dawn clear up, but I couldn't keep it to myself any longer.

" Dawn, have you got a minute" I asked," yep, you look worried, what's up " , she asked," I got something to show you, come with me" ,I said and gestured the way to the front lounge area," what do you see out the window", I asked," umm, cloudy sky, couple of cars, a few people, what am I supposed to be looking at" she asked," three ford galaxy's with blacked out windows", said a young voice from behind us, it was Toni, " don't you need worry about them" I said to her," well going on your reactions and body language it seems like to me that they may be involved somehow in mums death and probably Barry's too", I looked round to see if anyone was listening, nobody else was in the room, "we will tell you, but you must never tell anyone, not even your brother"," dad, I'm fourteen, I'm not a kid anymore," Toni said in frustration," "ok, we will tell you later when Tom and Brian have gone to bed".

I looked out the window to find the cars and drivers had gone," we both saw them Dawn" Toni said reassuringly," I'm sure you did, " said Dawn," let's get the boys and go home, it's been a long day and there's nothing we can do at the moment", I said.

We got the boys and was home in about fifteen minutes, there was complete silence in the car, with none of us not knowing what to say.

We all went back to number sixteen, I call it that now, rather than our house or my house, which just doesn't sound right, Tom asked if Brian could have a sleep over and both Dawn and myself agreed and I asked Toni if Dawn could stay the night in Toni's room in the spare bed, Dawn thanked us both and said she didn't want to go back to an empty house tonight.

We didn't eat much at the hotel, as we were talking to friends and family most of the time, So we made the boys some sandwiches and secretly ordered a couple of pizzas for the three of us when the boys had gone to bed.

It was just after eight o'clock when we could see the boys were getting tired, so dawn and myself took the boys up to Toms bedroom and said goodnight.

The pizzas were promptly delivered at nine and we sat down with Toni to talk about the events of the day, our future and the puddle people and to see if we could help each other, Toni really does seem to have grown up over this past week, we got around to talking about the day's events and was just talking about school, Tom, Brian and work when the door bell rang.

"Who's that going to be at this time of night, today of all days" Dawn said, I answered the door, it was two men, one in a police uniform and one in an army uniform, I called Dawn to the door, we both stood there holding hands, more for comfort really than anything else.

We were stood there looking at the two gentleman and the three black ford galaxy's out on the road," sorry to bother you both, were here to let you know that two of our officers died today in a rather bizarre accident," what happened" I asked," it seems that both cars were going away from the crematorium towards the town and as they went through south street the two cars collided in a rather large puddle, both cars overturned and landed on their roofs and both men drowned, we were told by people caught up in the traffic jam that they were on their way to the grand hotel to pay their respects to both of you on the day of your partners funerals".

" Were sorry for the sad loss of your officers, but we didn't know either of them and can't understand how they knew mum and Barry and if you don't mind we would like to mourn our loss and try to rebuild our lives with our dad and new mum, "Toni said from behind us, then stepped forward and shut the door in their faces.

I looked at Toni and then back to Dawn and smiled, I held Toni and said thank you, we then went back into the lounge.

We sat down again and was just finishing the last of the pizza and talking about work when we heard a lot of noise and commotion from outside, we went to the window to have a look and there seemed to be three road sweepers, their yellow beacons switched off and only their sidelights on, going up and down the road, on to the pavement, along by peoples driveways, and anywhere else they could get access.

" Toni , look after the house for a few minutes, where just popping down the road" ,I said," ok dad" she replied.

Dawn and myself went down our road and right around the block, there were road sweepers everywhere, one, two, three in one road, up on the pavement along the edges of driveways," why the hell couldn't they have done this weeks ago, all that loss of life" Dawn said," I think it's because it's one of theirs has been killed this time", I said, we continued counting and with a bit of guess work we estimated there was as many as thirty road sweepers from all over the county.

We got back to number sixteen and saw no more puddles or red dust," I think it's over" dawn said as we reached the front door.

" I LOVE YOU" I SAID

17419877R00059

Printed in Poland
by Amazon Fulfillment
Poland Sp. z o.o., Wrocław